For Harvey

Copyright © 2001 Christyan and Diane Fox
All rights reserved · CIP Data is available
Published in the United States 2001 by Handprint Books, Inc.
413 Sixth Avenue, Brooklyn, New York 11215
www.handprintbooks.com

First American Edition
Originally published in Great Britain by Little Tiger Press
Printed in Singapore · ISBN 1-929766-16-5
2 4 6 8 10 9 7 5 3 1

Fire Fighter PiggyWiggy

Christyan and Diane Fox

Handprint Books ✋ Brooklyn, New York

Whenever I see a fire engine racing by, I dream of all the things that I would do if I were a fearless fire fighter.

I would wear
a big yellow hat
and slide down
a shiny pole
on my way to
an emergency...

a big red fire engine
and a screaming siren.

Maybe I could climb a tall ladder to rescue someone stuck in a very high place...

or save
someone
stuck down
a deep
dark hole.

blazing fires
powerful
hose.

But it's always that in a real

good to know emergency...